The Day the Dragon Danced

By Kay Haugaard • Illustrated by Carolyn Reed Barritt

Library of Congress Cataloging-in-Publication Data

Haugaard, Kay.
  The day the dragon danced / by Kay Haugaard ; illustrated by Carolyn
Reed Barritt.
        p. cm.
  Summary: An African American girl takes her grandmother to watch the
Chinese New Year's parade where her father is a member of the dragon
dance troupe, along with many other ethnically diverse friends of their
community.
  ISBN-13: 978-1-885008-30-5
  ISBN-10: 1-885008-30-9
  [1. Grandmothers--Fiction. 2. Chinese New Year--Fiction. 3. African
Americans--Fiction. 4. Race relations--Fiction.] I. Barritt, Carolyn
Reed, ill. II. Title.
  PZ7.H2865Day 2006
  [E]--dc22
                                              2006011555

Shen's Books
Fremont, California

Printed in China

Book Design and computer production: Patty Arnold, Menagerie Design and Publishing

Dedicated to Kirsten, Mark, Liana and Kelsi
—Kay Haugaard

To Matthew
—Carolyn Reed Barritt

"So what's a dragon got to do
with New Year's?
It isn't even New Year's.
Here it is February already."

Grandma was cranky 'cause she didn't want to go to the parade. I pulled her hand to make her go faster. I wanted to see the dragon dance.

"Dragons I read about weren't any too friendly," she said as we walked down toward Main Street.

"These are different dragons, Grandma. These are Chinese dragons. My teacher Miss Peng says they are wise and strong and chase away bad spirits or eat them up. That leaves all the good spirits for us. Then we'll have a good year."

I could see the booths set up all around the street now as we got closer. There were Chinese paintings and calendars in the booths and I could smell delicious things cooking. There were little tiny trees and bamboo in pots.

"That's what she says, hah?" said Grandma. "We didn't have Chinese New Year parades here in our town when I was a little girl. I never set eyes on a Chinese person 'til I was a grown woman. Now there's a Chinese restaurant on every corner."

Grandma kept talking to herself as we walked among the booths. "Now there's a Taco stand! That's not Chinese."

"Look, Grandma, this is dragon's beard candy. Can I have some? Miss Peng told us about it."

"All right, child."

"And a sesame seed bun?"

"I guess, long as we've come, but that's all, you hear?" I pulled Grandma over to the curb with the other people, then looked down the street for the dragon. The parade hadn't started yet. The dragon was going to dance in the New Year's parade.

"First it's your daddy going to that Kung Fu class and now it's Chinese New Year parades here in February. Things sure are changing. And when did New Year's Day start being in February?" Grandma grumbled.

"It's in February because the Chinese have a different calendar, Grandma. It's called a lunar calendar. That means it's based on the moon." I felt so smart to remember all the stuff we learned in school.

"Well, that's really something – you teaching me, honey."

"Can you remember what color Daddy's shoes are, Grandma?" I pulled on her hand.

"How d'you expect me to remember what color your daddy's shoes are, child? You're the smart little kid. You should be better remembering things than I am."

But suddenly I remembered something else Miss Peng had told us. "Chinese dragons can fly through the air without any wings. Did you know that, Grandma?"

"Your teacher said that too?"

"Yes."

There was a clanging sound. Metal hitting metal. "Sounds like the parade is starting!" I looked down the street. There were high school kids beating drums in time to clanging cymbals. They lifted their feet up and down like they were marching, but didn't move.

"See, the drums beat the rhythm for the dragon to dance to, Grandma. He welcomes in the first day of the New Year."

"He's going to dance? Well, I never saw a dragon dance."

Now things started coming down the street. A man driving a red convertible went by. He waved to everyone and threw chocolate candy money wrapped in bright gold foil. The red streamers on his car fluttered. There were Chinese words on them.

"You know what that says, Grandma?"

"I surely do not but let me guess. Could it say, 'Happy New Year?'"

"That's right. In Chinese you say, '*Gung hay fat choy*.'"

"Miss Peng told you that?"

"No, Daddy did. When is the dragon coming?"

All at once there were fire crackers
snapping and popping!

CRAAAK! Snap! Snap! Snap!
CRAKKKLE! POW!

I jumped about a foot.

"Oh, my heart!" cried Grandma.
Then she laughed.

A red fire truck with red and gold paper decorations snorted slowly down the road. A lot of pretty girls were on the truck. They wore bright golden satin dresses. Some had long black hair and some had brown and one had yellow. They smiled and waved and threw money into the street. I ran out to pick up a shiny new penny. "Here, Grandma," I said, handing it to her. "See, that means you'll have lots of money in the new year."

"I surely can use some of that, child." Grandma smiled and put the lucky penny in her purse. Then she rubbed me on the head.

But where was the Dragon?

A clang of cymbals announced the dragon.

"Grandma, look!"

The dragon's huge red, green, white and orange head came around the corner. His sharp white, teeth shone in his wide open mouth. His fierce red eyes looked from side to side. Below his chin hung his white beard.

"Look! Look!" I squealed.

The dragon raised his head high then made it low. His eyes rolled some more. "He's looking for bad things to eat up, Grandma." I giggled excitedly and grabbed Grandma's coat sleeve. The cymbals crashed and crashed for the dragon to keep time with his many, many feet.

"Better watch out, Child, you're pretty bad sometimes!" Quickly she grabbed me around the middle and I jumped.

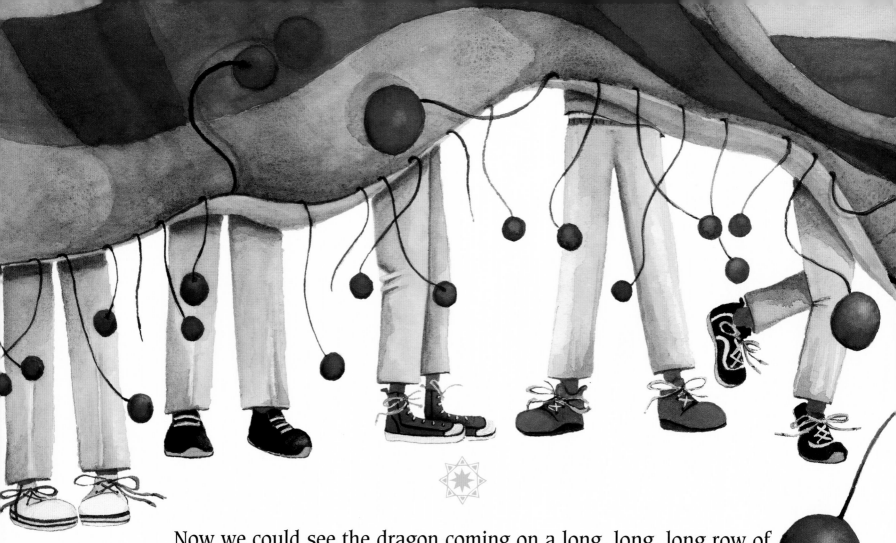

Now we could see the dragon coming on a long, long, long row of legs. They all had red socks but each pair ended in a different kind of athletic shoes. I watched the feet carefully.

The dragon had

white shoes with black trim

black shoes with white trim

white shoes with red trim

black shoes with red trim

red shoes with black trim

plain black shoes

plain white

and even plain red shoes.

What a long, long, LONG dragon he was. His bright red, green, and yellow cloth back curved like a stretched-out parasol held up by poles. The cymbals crashed again but the dragon didn't keep time. Some of his feet came down before the drum. Some came down after. The dragon was not dancing. He was stumbling. I watched the shoes carefully.

Boom! Boom! Boom! went the drums.
The dragon's back went up and his back
went down. But it was bumpy,
not smooth like a dragon should be.
Gongs clanged, drums banged,
feet went up, and feet went down
all at the wrong times.

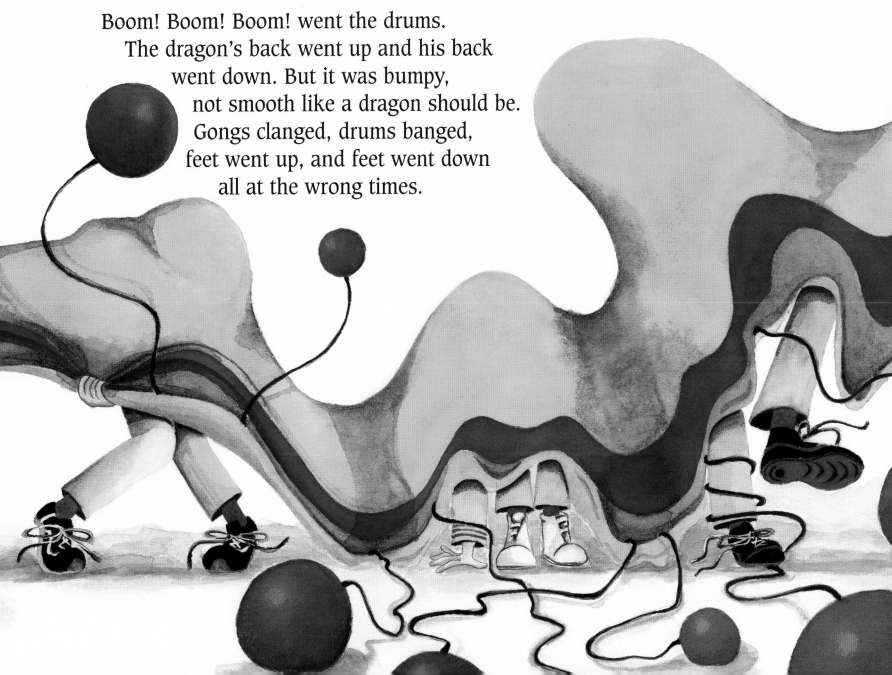

"Why doesn't he dance, Grandma? He isn't even walking very well and I can't tell which shoes..." I frowned at Grandma. She frowned back. "Look," I said, "his feet all do different things."

Then the dragon stopped. His tail was right beside us and there I saw Daddy's shoes. Now I remembered. He had red shoelaces. There they were, dragging on the pavement. All the feet went up and down in place. "Look, Grandma, there are Daddy's shoes and his laces are untied."

"Run quick," Grandma urged. "Go tie them."

Running into the street I slipped under the dragon and tied Daddy's shoelaces. Then, quickly I smiled up at Daddy and he smiled at me. Both of his hands were on a stick holding up the dragon's tail. Then his mouth said thanks but he made no sound.

When I ran back to the curb the dragon started again. The fringe on his body shook like he was getting ready to do something. He curved clear from side to side of the street but he didn't dance yet.

Gradually the dragon's legs started working together. He jumped on one side, then the other. Clang, clang, boom, boom went the cymbals and drum. It was almost a dance. His long body rippled up and down like bright sunset waves. He bounced back and forth with the drums. His front feet turned to one side then to the other.

He raised his huge head to all the people. He waved his pointed tail in the air. He rolled his red eyes and showed his pointed teeth. His mouth was big enough to swallow the sun. The dragon was dancing.

"Now isn't that something." Grandma laughed as she bounced back and forth too.

"See, Grandma, see, he's following the sun."

"Sun, hah? That fancy red ball thing that man's holding on a stick?"

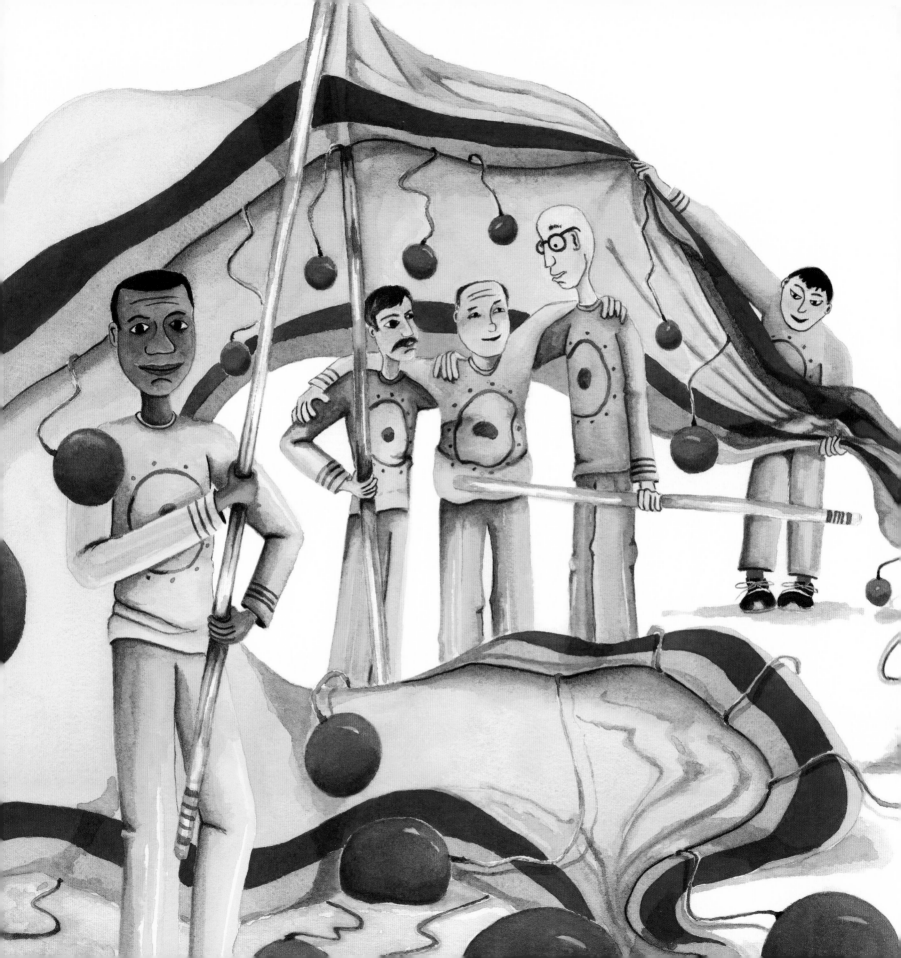

Grandma and I followed the dragon as he wiggled and danced all the way down the block and around the corner. The dragon danced right into a parking lot and stopped. Then out stepped my daddy, Mr. Chu who has the grocery store on the corner, Mr. Johnson who has the barber shop, Mr. Feng who owns the video store, Mr. Gonzalez who teaches fifth grade at our school, and Dr. Ito, who fixes my teeth.

They all wore yellow satin suits and red socks and athletic shoes.

Everyone was removing the poles they used to hold up the dragon. I ran over to Daddy and he stooped down and hugged me. "The dragon didn't dance together so well at first," I said to him.

"That's all right, Sugar," said Daddy, "we did pretty well just starting out. It takes a while to learn to dance together."

Grandma came up behind me and smiled at everyone.

"Happy New Year," she said, "*Gung hay fat choy.*"

Grandma and I followed the dragon as he wiggled and danced all the way down the block and around the corner. The dragon danced right into a parking lot and stopped. Then out stepped my daddy, Mr. Chu who has the grocery store on the corner, Mr. Johnson who has the barber shop, Mr. Feng who owns the video store, Mr. Gonzalez who teaches fifth grade at our school, and Dr. Ito, who fixes my teeth.

They all wore yellow satin suits and red socks and athletic shoes.

Everyone was removing the poles they used to hold up the dragon. I ran over to Daddy and he stooped down and hugged me. "The dragon didn't dance together so well at first," I said to him.

"That's all right, Sugar," said Daddy, "we did pretty well just starting out. It takes a while to learn to dance together."

Grandma came up behind me and smiled at everyone.

"Happy New Year," she said, "*Gung hay fat choy*."